THE PRINCE AND THE PAUPER

THE PRINCE AND THE PAUPER

MARK TWAIN

Retold by
Raymond James

Illustrated by
S.D. Schindler

Troll Associates

Library of Congress Cataloging-in-Publication Data

James, Raymond.
    Prince and the pauper / by Mark Twain; retold by Raymond James;
illustrated by S.D. Schindler.
        p.   cm.—(Troll illustrated classics)
    Summary: When young Edward VI of England and a poor boy who
resembles him exchange places, each learns something about the
other's very different station in life.
    ISBN 0-8167-1873-3 (lib. bdg.)   ISBN 0-8167-1874-1 (pbk.)
    1. Edward VI, King of England, 1537-1553—Juvenile fiction.
[1. Edward VI, King of England, 1537-1553—Fiction. 2. Adventure
and adventurers—Fiction. 3. England—Fiction.] I. Schindler,
S.D., ill. II. Twain, Mark, 1835-1910. Prince and the pauper.
III. Title.
PZ7.J1543Pr 1990
[Fic]—dc20   89-33892

Tom Canty knew he was late. The young boy ran through the dark, narrow streets to get home. The slums of London were bad enough in warm weather. But in winter, they were almost unbearable. It was so cold that tears formed in the corners of Tom's eyes. The icy wind had already turned his ears bright red. His hands, feet, and face were frozen.

Just ahead lay Offal Court. That was where his family lived. Father, mother, two sisters, and Tom shared just one room on the third floor of a small, rickety, decayed house. Other families just as poor as the Cantys were crammed into the rest of the house.

Tom stopped in front of it. He pulled his ragged coat tighter around him. No coins jingled in his coat pockets. The day had been a disaster for begging—not a penny made. Tom shuddered at the thought of what his father would do when he found out. Slowly, Tom climbed the creaking wooden stairs to the third floor. As soon as he entered the door, John Canty grabbed his son by the collar.

"Well? Where is it? Come on!" boomed John Canty. He cuffed Tom sharply across one of his cold-reddened ears. The blow stung like a bee. "What? Have you not a penny? By gad, boy, you *better* have if you know what's good for you!"

"I . . . I . . . I didn't make any money today, Father," said Tom, rubbing his ear.

"Oh, no?" said his father angrily. "Did you beg in the streets as I told you to?" John Canty took Tom's other ear and yanked it. "Well? ANSWER ME!" The slap from his father's hand knocked Tom to the floor. When he regained his feet, Tom was slapped again by his father.

In the corner, trembling with fear, were Tom's mother and his two sisters, Bet and Nan. But Mrs. Canty could not remain still for long while her boy was being hit. She ran between father and son. "Please, John, let him be!"

Then helplessly, she went back to her two daughters in the corner. There, they watched tearfully as John Canty beat his son. When he was finished, John Canty packed the boy off to bed without any supper.

In the filthy straw that served as his bed, Tom bit his fist. He wouldn't give his father the satisfaction of hearing him cry. Later, when John Canty fell asleep, Tom's mother sneaked some crusts of bread to him in bed. Tom looked at her with thankful eyes. He loved his mother dearly. Tom knew she was taking a chance. If she got caught giving him food, she would also be beaten.

The misery of his life, of begging in the streets, of being thrashed by his father, only stopped when Tom was asleep. Then, he would dream about giants and fairies, dwarves and genies, kings and princes. These he learned about from the stories told by Father Andrew. He was a priest who now lived in the same house as the Cantys, but had once lived in the king's palace. Somehow, Father Andrew had angered the king, who dismissed him and left him penniless. But the priest was a good, kind man who taught Tom how to read and write.

Father Andrew's tales of bold, handsome princes only increased Tom's desire to see a real prince. Throughout the winter and into spring, Tom could hardly think of anything else. Soon he was even *acting* like a prince. His speech and manners had a royal air about them. Some people mocked Tom. But others grew to respect his judgment. Tom was becoming something of a hero to nearly everyone in Offal Court except his family. They saw nothing special in him at all.

One day, after earning a couple of coins begging in the streets, Tom wandered close to the royal palace. He marveled at the splendor of the huge stone buildings, the well-kept grounds, and the guards dressed in rich plumage. Tom wedged his way through the crowd that always gathered just outside the palace gates. When he got to the gilt bars of the fence, he saw something that almost made him shout for joy.

Inside the palace gates was a boy clothed in silks and satins. He was wearing a little jeweled sword on his hip and a jaunty cap on his head. Surrounding him were many servants, all attending to his every need. A prince! thought Tom. A real prince—just as I imagined!

10

Tom didn't see one of the guards approach him from the side. His face was still pressed against the bars of the fence when the guard snatched him rudely away. Tom was sent sprawling backward into the crowd.

"Mind your manners, young beggar!" said the guard gruffly.

The crowd laughed. But the young prince inside the gates saw what had happened and rushed toward the guard.

"How dare you abuse this poor lad, soldier!" said the prince. "Open the gates and let him in!"

The guard did as the prince commanded. The crowd parted to make way for the pauper who now passed through the gates. The prince took the boy's hand and led him toward the palace.

"I'm Edward Tudor, Prince of Wales, son of King Henry the Eighth," said the prince. "You look tired and hungry. Come with me."

Edward brought Tom to a magnificent room inside the palace. The prince ordered that food be brought for Tom. Then Edward waved away his servants, leaving the two boys alone.

"What's your name, lad?" the prince asked.

"Tom, Your Grace. Uh, Tom Canty."

"Where do you live?"

"In the city, sir. Offal Court."

"Offal Court! That's an odd place to live," said the prince. "Have you parents?"

"Yes, Your Grace. And two sisters besides."

"Do your parents treat you well?"

"My mother is truly a saint, Your Grace," answered Tom. He paused, then continued. "My father, um, only beats me when he's drunk or awake."

"*Beats* you, you say?" exclaimed the prince, shocked. "And you so frail and little! Why, before the day is out, I'll have my father command that he be taken to the Tower where—"

"Pardon, Your Grace," interrupted Tom, "but the Tower is for those of high rank. My father is but a poor man of low station."

"Hmmm, right you are, lad," said the prince. "How old are your sisters?"

"Bet and Nan are both fifteen, Your Grace."

"Why, my own sister, Princess Elizabeth, is just a year younger than yours. And Lady Jane Grey, my cousin, is my own age. You look to be about my age, too. Now, tell me more about this Offal Court."

"Well, Your Grace, in summer we swim in the canals and in the river. And we race each other in the streets. Sometimes we play in the sand, covering each other up. And sometimes we make mud pies and fling them at each other!"

"Oh, marvelous! Marvelous!" said the prince gleefully. "I wish I could do that. Just once, I'd like to strip these royal garments off, dress like you, and roll in the mud!"

"And I, Your Grace, have often dreamed of being dressed like you," said Tom sheepishly.

"Why, then, let's do it!" said Edward, clapping his hands together in joy. "We'll trade clothes before anyone else comes to my room. Come on, lad. Give me your coat."

And so the two boys exchanged clothing. Soon Edward was dressed in dirty, torn shoes, shirt, and coat. Tom, on the other hand, was beaming at himself in the mirror. From head to foot, he was adorned in the rich clothes of a real prince. Standing side by side, the two boys both looked in the mirror. What they saw surprised them both.

"Well, well," said Edward. "Do you see what I see, Tom?"

"Your Grace, I dare not say it."

"Then I will say it for you, lad," said the prince. "You have the same hair, eyes, voice, manner, face, height, and look as I have. Why, we could pass as twins! I even feel the way you must have felt when that soldier—say, what's that on your hand?"

"Oh, just a little bruise, Your Grace. Nothing to trouble yourself over. I must have done it trying to break my fall."

"It's that guard at the gates!" fumed Edward. "What he did was shameful and cruel. Wait here. I intend to have a further word with him about his behavior."

The prince snatched something from a table, hid it, and then hurried out of the room. He dashed down the hall and outside toward the gates. The guard who mistreated Tom was standing outside them.

"Open these gates at once!" commanded Edward.

The guard did as he was told. But as the prince went through the gates, the soldier knocked him to the ground.

"Take that, you little beggar, for getting me into trouble with His Highness!"

The crowd roared with laughter. Edward picked himself up. He was covered in mud. Enraged, he said, "I am the Prince of Wales, you dog! My person is sacred. You shall hang for laying a hand on me!"

The guard gave Edward a mock salute. "I am your obedient servant, Your Noble Highness." Then the soldier kicked Edward in the seat of his pants. "Be off with you!"

The crowd closed in around Edward now. They hustled him down the road, hooting and hollering. "Make way for His Royal Grace!" they yelled, laughing. "Make way for the Prince of Wales!" Edward could not make himself heard above the mob's taunts and shouts. The heir to the English throne was being treated no better than a common beggar.

The prince's luck only got worse when the crowd abandoned him in front of Christ's Church Hospital. This was a home for poor, deserted children. And some of them, seeing the mud-spattered rags Edward was wearing, decided he needed a bath. They dunked him in a nearby horse pond. Emerging drenched, Edward was then attacked by a pack of dogs. By the time he freed himself, he was bruised and bleeding.

Suddenly, a rough hand seized Edward from behind and led him through a maze of dirty alleyways and foul-smelling streets. The hand belonged to John Canty. He promised the boy the thrashing of his life when they got home to Offal Court. Edward, however, kept insisting he was not his son.

Finally, John Canty lost his patience. He raised his walking stick to drum some sense into the boy. But the arm of a bystander stopped him. Incensed, John Canty brought the heavy stick down upon the head of the meddler. The man groaned, then slumped to the ground. Blood oozed from his skull. But John Canty did not recognize the man nor did he stop to help him. He pulled Edward on through the streets. And when the boy claimed he was the Prince of Wales, John Canty thought his son was stark raving mad!

Left alone in the prince's room, Tom Canty began to worry. It had been a few hours since Edward Tudor departed. What if someone discovers me in the prince's clothes—in the prince's own room? thought Tom. I'll hang for sure!

Without warning, the door to the room swung open. Tom was prepared to greet Edward when he saw a servant instead. "Lady Jane Grey is here to see you, Your Grace," announced the servant. Then a pretty young girl entered the room.

"Hello, My Lord," she said softly to Tom.

Stammering, Tom said, "P-P-Please, Your Ladyship, be merciful! In truth, I am no lord at all, but poor Tom Canty of Offal Court. Spare me my life, I beg of you!"

Lady Jane Grey was startled. And when Tom knelt before her, she shrieked and ran from the room. She went immediately to her uncle, the king, and told him that his son was not in his right mind. King Henry listened to his niece, then sent a servant to bring his son to his chamber.

Tom's actions in front of the king were just as "crazy" as before. He insisted he wasn't the prince at all, but one Tom Canty. Then he begged for his life again, asking for mercy.

King Henry sat there, perplexed. What was the matter with his son, the prince? After talking with the court physicians, the king concluded Prince Edward was overtired from his studies. The king commanded they stop at once. He also commanded the entire palace household to act no differently in front of the prince. Edward's ravings were temporary, believed King Henry, and should therefore be ignored.

The Earl of Hertford and Lord St. John hated to see their young master so confused. Then and there, the two decided to help the prince in every way they could. They would guide him through the duties of his royal office until he got better.

"Perhaps tonight's banquet at the Lord Mayor's residence will restore your old self, Your Grace," said Lord St. John.

Banquet? thought Tom. He felt he was getting deeper and deeper into trouble. Tom wondered how long it would take before everyone saw through him.

Yet no one questioned his odd table manners that night at the Lord Mayor's. Tom ate with his fingers. He ordered that the beautiful linen napkin laid on his lap be removed "before food gets on it." He filled his pockets with nuts to munch on later in his room. Then, after he finished eating, Tom was presented with a golden dish of rose water to wash his hands. He looked at the dish, looked up at the servant holding it, and finally took it from him. As everyone in the dining hall watched, Tom tipped the dish toward his mouth and gulped down the rose water. Wiping his lips on his royal sleeve, he said, "Not bad, but it smells better than it tastes."

Tom was relieved when he was left alone in the prince's room. He jumped into bed and took out the nuts from his pockets. He looked around for something to crack them open with. In a suit of armor hanging from a wall, Tom found a small, round, gold object with swirls set in its flat part. Using it to crack the nuts open, Tom happily munched away. Then he swept the shells off the royal bedspread and under the royal bed, and went to sleep.

In the days that followed, Tom slowly adjusted to the life of a prince. In the beginning, he protested loud and long. But no one believed he wasn't the prince. And Tom *was* becoming fond of all the comforts and riches, though he felt four hundred servants were a bit too many for him. He still could not get used to someone washing him, another dressing him, another serving him food, another pouring him drinks, and another even taking whippings for him.

Tom's personal whipping boy, Humphrey Marlow, was *paid* to be beaten every time the prince stumbled in his studies. When the king ordered the prince's studies halted, the whipping boy pleaded with Tom to resume them. The only way Humphrey could earn enough money to support his poor mother and sister was by being beaten. Tom told him he'd start studying without telling the king. This cheered Humphrey, who thanked Tom and left with a big smile on his face.

Some time later, King Henry asked Tom if he recalled where he put the Great Seal of England that the king had given him. Puzzled, Tom said he knew nothing about it. But the king excused the boy once more, saying the prince's wits were failing him again. Every time Tom made a mistake, couldn't remember, or seemed out of sorts, his ''illness'' was blamed. And each time, Tom wondered what had happened to the *real* Prince of Wales.

I told you before and I'm telling you now—I am Edward, Prince of Wales, and none other!''

John Canty, his wife, and his two daughters didn't know what to make of the boy's words. They all agreed, though, that he must be out of his mind.

''Please, Tom,'' said Mrs. Canty, ''you're breaking my heart. Am I not your mother, who bore you and loves you still?''

Edward shook his head. ''Believe me, my good woman, I do not want to grieve you. But I tell you true, you are not my mother. I have never seen you before.'' The boy's eyes swept across all the Canty faces in the room. ''I have never seen *any* of you before.''

''Deny your own father, will you?'' bellowed John Canty. He rushed at Edward and began hitting him. Mrs. Canty and her two daughters retreated to the corner. But then Mrs. Canty could stand it no longer. She got up and tried to protect Edward from the beating. John Canty shoved her away. Then he continued thrashing Edward. When he finished, John Canty stormed over to his wife and daughters.

''Now,'' ordered John Canty, ''the lot of you get to bed. I don't want to hear a peep from any of you!''

Later that night, as her family slept, Mrs. Canty couldn't shake the feeling that maybe, just maybe, Tom wasn't Tom after all. And so she decided to test the boy. She knew Tom always reacted to surprise by holding his hands palm outwards in front of his eyes. He did this when he was startled from sleep or from daydreaming.

Mrs. Canty crept quietly over to the sleeping boy. Lighting a candle, she flashed it directly into his eyes. He awoke with a jump. But he made no hand gesture at all. Mrs. Canty surprised him twice more. Each time, the boy's eyes popped open. But his hands remained motionless. Mrs. Canty was confused. But she was also desperate. Out of concern for the boy's welfare, she forced herself to believe that he *must* be her son, Tom.

Mrs. Canty went back to her bed. The only sound in the room was that of her husband snoring loudly. She was drifting off to sleep when there were several sharp raps at the door.

"Who dares knock at this ungodly hour?" shouted John Canty, half-awake, from his bed.

A voice answered, "I've news, John Canty. That man you clubbed in the streets is dead. It was the priest, Father Andrew. If I were you, I wouldn't tarry in this place a minute longer. The police will be around for you—and it'll be the gallows that follow, sure enough."

John Canty got out of bed and woke his family. "Get up, all of you! We must flee right now! My neck's at stake!"

The family packed a few belongings and then burst out of the room and down the stairs. John Canty, holding tightly to Edward's wrist, told his family to meet at London Bridge if they should get separated. Then off they went.

But no sooner did the Cantys and Edward come near the Thames River than a huge procession of people engulfed them. They were singing and dancing in the streets. John Canty yelled for his family to go back. But it was too late. They were jostled apart by the crowd. Only John Canty and Edward remained together.

"Come on, boy," John Canty ordered Edward. "Keep up!"

A large hand fell on John Canty's shoulder, stopping him. "Not so fast, friend." It was one of the soldiers guarding the river. "Surely you're not in such a hurry that you can't drink to the health of our beloved Prince Edward!" The soldier shoved a cup full of rum toward Canty.

Not a man to turn down free liquor, John Canty loosened his grip on Edward to take a drink from the cup. At that moment, Edward darted into the crowd surrounding them. John Canty screamed after him, "Come back here, boy! Come back this second or I'll tan your hide proper!"

Edward ignored Canty and made straight for Guildhall. There, he intended to make himself known, denounce the impostor, and end this nightmare. Edward ran as fast as he could. When he got to the gates of Guildhall, he clamored to be admitted. "Let me pass! I am Edward, Prince of Wales! I will not be driven off from what is rightfully mine. I *demand* entrance!"

The crowd in front of Guildhall turned ugly. They were in a mood to celebrate, and this seedy-looking boy's shouts annoyed them. They ringed Edward and threatened him. "Take the beggar! Throw him in the horse pond! Drown the little rat!"

But before any of the mob could lay a finger on Edward, a tall, muscular man dressed in elegant though faded clothes stepped beside him. When someone grabbed the boy's arm, the man drew his sword and hit the person with its flat side.

"Kill him! Kill them both!" shouted angry voices from the crowd.

Keeping Edward by his side, the man held the mob at bay with his sword. Still, the crowd pressed closer and closer. Just when it seemed the two would be overcome, a voice shouted, "Make way for the king's messenger!" The mob parted to let a man on horseback approach the gates of Guildhall. That same instant, the man with the sword managed to lead Edward away from danger. But before the boy left, he heard a whisper pass between the messenger and the guard at the gates. "King Henry is dead! Prince Edward is now king!"

W hat?'' asked Tom Canty in shock. He was sitting in bed, cracking nuts and popping them in his mouth. A servant was standing before him.

''Your Majesty, I asked if you will be giving your commands now,'' said the servant.

''Commands? What are you talking about?'' asked Tom.

''Sire, surely you've heard,'' replied the servant, bowing his head. ''Your father, King Henry, passed away earlier today. Last night, you were Edward, Prince of Wales. Today, you are Edward, King of England!'' The servant knelt on one knee.

A walnut fell from Tom's lips. His eyes bulged and his hands shook. Playing prince was one thing, thought Tom. But playing *king* was something else entirely. Where will this end? he wondered.

Both the Earl of Hertford and Lord St. John entered Tom's room soon after the servant left. The two men consoled the boy over the loss of his father, the king. But they urged him to put grief out of his heart for the time being and tackle his first day's duties as King of England.

''Uh, what should the king do first today?'' asked Tom in a voice that didn't even convince himself.

"Why, if it please Your Majesty, the foreign ambassadors are waiting outside to see you," said the Earl of Hertford.

Tom saw them. The Earl of Hertford and Lord St. John helped him through the day. In fact, they helped the new king through the next several days. But Tom quickly got bored with the duties of being king.

On his fourth day as king, Tom wandered over to a window as an ambassador droned on and on about why he had come. Through the window, Tom could see a crowd trailing a wagon. On it stood a man, a woman, and a young girl. "What's going on down there?" Tom asked Lord St. John.

"Sire, the three are to be executed for crimes against the realm. They're being led to the gallows."

"Bring them here!" commanded Tom before he knew what he was saying.

Lord St. John ordered one of the soldiers to bring the condemned prisoners to the king's chamber. Minutes later, the man, woman, and young girl were brought in. All three were bound in heavy chains. They were accompanied by one of the executioner's guards.

"What crimes have they committed?" asked Tom.

"The man, Sire, has been convicted of poisoning another man in Islington," answered the guard.

"This was proven?" asked Tom.

"It was, Your Majesty," replied the guard. "A witch had foretold that the victim would die by poison. The poisoner would be a man with brown hair and clothed in a worn coat. This man has both brown hair and a worn coat, Sire. And he was seen leaving the victim's house an hour before the body was found."

"Well, man," said Tom, "what do you say to that?"

"I am innocent, Sire," replied the man. "I was miles away from Islington at the time of the man's death. They say I was inside his house *taking* a life. But Sire, I was actually *saving* a life. I pulled a drowning boy from the Thames River."

Hearing this, Tom perked up. He remembered Father Andrew telling him how a man had saved a boy, an Offal Court lad, from drowning. The boy's name was—what? Tom tried to remember. Witt! It suddenly came back to him. "What was the drowning boy's name?" Tom asked the prisoner.

"He said his name was Giles, Your Majesty. Giles Witt." The condemned man's shoulders drooped. It was as if he had given up all hope of justice—or mercy.

"This prisoner is innocent. Let him go free. It is the king's will!" said Tom. "I will have no one in my kingdom hanged on such flimsy evidence!"

A low buzz of admiration could be heard throughout the king's chamber now. The wisdom of Tom's decision and the mercy he showed impressed everyone there. "This is no mad king," whispered one onlooker, "but a king most sane and wise!" Another agreed. "He has acted just like his own father. A true king!"

But Tom was not finished. "What are the crimes of this woman and girl?" he asked.

"Crimes most foul, Your Majesty," replied the guard. "This mother and her daughter sold their souls to the devil. It was proven, and they were sentenced to hang in accordance with the law of the realm."

"How was this proven?" asked Tom.

"Sire, forty witnesses have sworn that the evil power these two received was used to destroy the village they lived in. They conjured up a storm that wasted the land around them."

"Did the two also suffer in this storm?"

"They did, Sire."

"And how did they bring about this storm?"

"According to the witnesses, Sire, by pulling off their stockings."

"Does a storm always follow the removal of their stockings?"

"So it is said, Your Majesty."

Tom now turned to the two prisoners in front of him. The little girl could not have been any older than nine. "Do your worst! I command you both to bring about a storm!"

The king's servants paled at this command. Fear rippled through some of the king's advisers, too. But Tom remained calm.

"Remove your stockings! I wish to see a storm!" he commanded again.

The two prisoners did as the king ordered. They removed their stockings. A few servants ducked behind some draperies. They were afraid that violent winds, lightning, and huge hailstones would suddenly tear the place apart. But nothing happened.

Tom walked closer to the mother. "Make a storm, woman, and I'll spare your lives! Fail, and you'll both be put to death!"

The mother dropped to her knees, holding her hands out before her. "Please, Sire, spare the life of my little girl. I cannot do as you command. I have been falsely accused. But I'd gladly lose my life to save my daughter's. I beg of you, take me, not my little girl!" The woman was sobbing.

The sweet, kind face of his own mother came back to Tom now. He was almost moved to tears himself. "Rise, good woman. Only a mother who loved her child above herself would speak as you spoke. If you had the evil power they said you have, you would have used it to save your daughter's life. Trouble yourself no further. Take your little girl and go your way in peace. No harm shall come to either of you." Tom looked up at everyone present in the chamber. He spoke so that all could hear him clearly. "These prisoners are to be set free at once—by order of the king!"

Long live King Edward the Sixth!"

This cry took Edward by surprise as the man with the sword led him through London's streets. Word of King Henry's death spread quickly throughout England. Edward was still sad about the loss of his father. Why, I'm king now, he thought. How strange it is to be king . . . and yet *not* king!

Edward told the man with the sword that he, Edward, was England's true and rightful king. But the man looked at him with the same pitying eyes he showed the boy outside Guildhall. When Edward finished telling his story, the man, named Miles Hendon, told his.

Miles' father was Sir Richard Hendon, a baronet who lived at Hendon Hall in Kent. Sir Richard had three sons. Arthur, the oldest, was kind and generous. Miles came next. He was also good-hearted, though wild and sometimes hotheaded. Hugh, the youngest, was a vile, cruel boy who hated his two older brothers. Their mother died giving birth to Hugh. Besides the father and three boys, there was a cousin, Lady Edith. Heiress to a great fortune, she was a beautiful, gentle girl placed in the care of Sir Richard after her own parents had passed away.

Miles' younger brother, Hugh, did everything he could to turn his father against the other two boys. When Arthur died suddenly from poor health, that meant Hugh had only Miles to contend with. And Hugh told lies about Miles, saying he intended to marry Lady Edith without seeking Sir Richard's blessing. Hugh hoped to wed his cousin himself, not because he loved her as Miles did, but because he wanted her fortune.

Sir Richard believed the lies Hugh told about Miles. Angry, the father told Miles he could not return to Hendon Hall for three years. Sir Richard hoped Miles would become a soldier and make a man of himself in that time. Then he could come back to Hendon Hall.

Heartbroken, Miles did as his father wished. He left and joined the king's army. For three years, he fought in the continental wars. But in his last battle, Miles was taken prisoner. Thrown into a dungeon, Miles was kept locked up for the next seven years. Finally, he managed to escape. Only recently had he arrived back in London. Miles was on his way to Hendon Hall. When he passed by Guildhall, he saw young Edward being set upon by the mob. That was when he jumped in and rescued the boy.

"You have been shamefully abused!" said Edward. "And you have saved my life. Such an act will not go unrewarded. Kneel before me." Flustered, Miles did as the boy commanded. "By the power of the king, I dub you a knight of the realm. Rise, *Sir* Miles Hendon." Miles stood up, still flushed in the face. "I promise to make things right for you again, Sir Miles. The king has said it!"

Miles thought the boy had completely lost his wits. Yet the man's heart went out to him. Poor, ruined, little fellow, thought Miles. I will be your friend and protector until you are better.

"Come, uh, Sire, let's travel to Hendon Hall. There's no place else for us to go."

With the little money Miles had, he bought a mule for himself and a donkey for the boy. They rode together at a casual pace. Miles did not want to tire the boy. He worried that the lad's condition might get worse.

All along the way, Miles told Edward about his father and Lady Edith. Miles' spirits were soaring. He was eager to be home again, and he imagined the warm welcome he'd get there. Miles especially wanted to see his beloved cousin again. He had sorely missed her these past ten years. His love for her was as strong as ever.

"There it is! Just ahead!" shouted Miles, pointing to a huge mansion. As they passed through the stone gateway, Miles could barely restrain himself. "Ah, what a great day! My father and brother and Lady Edith will all be wild with joy at the sight of me! I just know it!" Miles spurred his mule to move a little faster. Edward kept up as best as he could on the donkey.

When they reached the mansion, Miles jumped down from his mule and helped Edward down from the donkey. Then Miles ushered the boy into the house. The two entered a large room where a man sat before a roaring fire.

"Stand and greet your long-lost brother, Hugh!" Miles exclaimed. "It's me, Miles! And call our father and tell him I have returned."

Hugh stood up. But instead of coming toward Miles, he stepped back. "Who are you, stranger?"

"Why, I am your older brother," said Miles, a little uneasily. "Surely you'd recognize your own brother?"

"That I would, sir," replied Hugh. "But both my brothers are dead. My oldest brother, Arthur, died when I was still young. And my other brother, Miles, died in battle. We received a letter informing us of his death seven years ago."

A dark look crept over Miles' face. "That's a lie!" said Miles sharply. Then, calming himself, he said, "Call Father. He will know me."

"One cannot call the dead, sir."

"Dead?" Miles' voice was soft now. "My father—dead?" Stunned, Miles mumbled, "Please do not say that Lady Edith— "

"Is dead?" interrupted Hugh, finishing the sentence for Miles. "No. She lives."

"Saints be praised!" said Miles, relieved. "Please, Hugh, summon her here. She will know me. She will recognize me."

Hugh left the room. Miles began pacing the floor, muttering to himself. Then he turned to Edward, who was standing off to the side. "Believe me, Sire, I am no impostor! I was born here, raised here, loved here. Please, do not doubt me."

"I do not doubt you, Sir Miles," said Edward.

"I thank you from my heart," said Miles. He was genuinely moved by the boy's faith in him.

"Do you doubt *me*?" asked Edward. He looked directly into Miles' eyes.

A guilty feeling came over Miles at the boy's question. But before he could reply, the door to the room swung open. A beautiful lady walked in, with Hugh behind her. It was Lady Edith. Her head was bowed, and her face was very sad.

"Look at this man," said Hugh, pointing to Miles. "Do you know him?"

The blood drained from Lady Edith's face as she answered. "No, I do not know him." Then, without another word, she turned and left the room.

Stunned, Miles slumped into a chair. He was speechless.

"There you have it, sir," said Hugh. "You heard my wife say she does not know you. Now, if you and the boy would kindly leave—"

"WIFE!" exploded Miles. In an instant, he had Hugh by the throat and was throttling him. "Fox-hearted villain, it was *you* who wrote that lying letter! It was *you* who stole my true love from me!" Miles almost choked Hugh to death before loosening his grip. "Away with you, scoundrel! I won't dirty my hands killing you!"

Hugh stumbled backward, gasping for breath. Then he bolted through the door for help. A few moments later, a group of soldiers rushed in. They quickly overpowered Miles and chained him. Edward was also taken and bound. Then the two were dragged from Hendon Hall. Behind them, Miles and Edward could hear Hugh chuckling and Lady Edith crying.

In jail, Miles was visited by Blake Andrews, one of the older servants at Hendon Hall. The jailer opened the cell for Andrews. With the jailer still within earshot, Andrews mocked and insulted Miles. Then, when the jailer went back to his post, Andrews' tone of voice changed dramatically. "It *is* you, my master. I believed you were dead these seven years past. And lo, here you are! I knew who you were the moment I saw you at Hendon Hall!"

Miles sneered. "Then why didn't you speak up when you had the chance?"

"I could not," replied Andrews. "Your brother, Sir Hugh, is a cruel tyrant who tolerates no disobedience and demands total loyalty from his servants. If I spoke, I would have been whipped and put out of the house without a penny. I have a wife and children to think of."

Then Andrews told Miles what had happened at Hendon Hall after the first three years of his absence. Sir Richard's health failed rapidly. He wanted to see Hugh and Edith settled in life before he died. But Edith begged hard for a month's delay, hoping Miles would return by then. When the month was up, she asked for another. At the end of the second month, the letter came, announcing Miles' death in battle. The shock gave Sir Richard a heart attack. He was truly sorry that he had ever sent Miles away. On his deathbed, Sir Richard insisted Edith marry Hugh. And so, as Sir Richard slipped into unconsciousness for the last time, the marriage took place by his bedside.

It was not a happy marriage. Shortly after the ceremony, Lady Edith found among her husband's papers several rough drafts of the letter announcing Miles' death. She accused Hugh of deceiving Sir Richard and herself. But Hugh just laughed. He told Lady Edith to mind her manners in his presence. She was his wife, and she would do what he told her to do. *Her* fortune was now *his* fortune.

"I have some other news, my lord," said Andrews. "It is rumored that the king is mad."

At this, Edward glared at the servant. "The king is *not* mad, good man. Do I *look* mad?"

34

Andrews darted a puzzled look at Miles. But Miles waved his fingers in front of his face, gesturing that the boy's outburst be ignored.

"The late king will be buried at Windsor in a day or two," continued Andrews. "Then the new king will be crowned at Westminster on the twentieth of this month."

"What?" said Edward. Here, Miles gestured for the boy to be quiet while the servant spoke.

"Sir Hugh will be at the coronation," said Andrews. "He has high hopes of being made a peer of the realm."

"And who would be stupid enough to make that black-hearted beetle a peer?" asked Edward in surprise.

"Why, the king himself!" answered Andrews.

"I would NEVER do such a thing!" shouted Edward.

"Boy, I am talking about our most serene highness, King Edward the Sixth!" said Andrews testily. "So mind your tongue! Whether the king be a little mad or not, his praises are on the lips of all his subjects. King Edward has struck down many unjust laws. He has shown great wisdom and mercy in his judgments. And I'll not have you show disrespect toward him now!"

Edward slumped down in the cell. Were his ears tricking him? Did this man just tell him that a beggar boy, a street urchin from one of London's foulest slums, was now winning the hearts of all Englishmen? In Edward's own clothes, in Edward's own palace, in Edward's own *name*? This was more than he could bear. Edward felt as if someone had robbed him—of himself!

The jailer returned. "Time's up," he said to Andrews. "I've orders to take these two before the magistrate for sentencing."

The magistrate did not take long. He sentenced Miles to two hours in the pillory for assuming a false identity and for attacking Sir Hugh Hendon. Edward was let off with just a warning.

Miles was hauled to the public square and placed in the stocks. His hands and head were locked into the holes. A crowd gathered around him. Edward had to push his way through. When he got to the front, Edward saw an egg sail through the air and splatter against Miles' cheek. The crowd roared with laughter as the yolk dripped from Miles' face. Then another egg shattered on Miles' head. The mob cheered.

"Stop at once!" shouted Edward, now facing the crowd. "Set this man free immediately! He is my servant. I am the—"

"Oh, peace, lad!" interrupted Miles from the stocks. "You'll destroy yourself." Then, raising his voice, Miles said, "Ignore the boy! He means no harm! He is mad!"

"Perhaps half a dozen lashes with a whip might restore the boy's wits," said Sir Hugh. He had just ridden up on his horse.

"Let the child go!" shouted Miles. "Heartless dogs! Can't you see how young and frail he is? Let him go! I'll take his lashes for him."

"Good idea," said Sir Hugh, smiling. Then he spoke to the soldier guarding Miles. "Let the little beggar go. And give this fellow in the stocks a dozen stripes across his back. Yes, an honest dozen—well laid on!"

The soldier stripped Miles to the waist in the pillory. He didn't make a sound as the soldier cut into his bare back twelve times with a whip. As each lash landed, Edward swore this loyal deed would never be forgotten.

After the soldier was finished, he tossed the whip away. He was ashamed of the punishment he was ordered to give. When the two hours were up, the soldier released Miles and hurried away.

Edward ran to Miles and hugged him. After treating the wounds on Miles' back, Edward brought the mule and donkey over.

"Where to, Sire?" asked Miles. His back ached.

"To London, Sir Miles," said Edward, leaping up on his donkey. "And to the coronation!"

All London was buzzing with excitement. It seemed everyone in the city had prepared for the coronation of King Edward the Sixth. Flowers lined the streets where the new king would travel up to Westminster Abbey to be crowned. Brightly colored streamers fluttered from rooftops and flagpoles. Shopkeepers had scrubbed and swept their stores spotless. The whole city had undergone a house-cleaning. Rarely had it looked so beautiful.

Tom Canty was excited, too. He still felt badly about the real prince. But as time wore on, and with Edward still absent, Tom became more involved in the duties of governing. He had done a great deal of good for the people of England. He was proud of that. So he looked on the coronation almost as if he *were* the rightful king who had *earned* the honor.

Dressed in the finest robes and jewels, Tom mounted a war steed and started out in front of a long procession. To his sides and behind him were the king's guard. They were followed by Lord St. John and the Earl of Hertford, Lady Jane Grey and Princess Elizabeth, and hundreds of other lords, ladies, earls, dukes, duchesses, and their retainers.

Slowly they moved through the streets of London, going from the Tower in the direction of Westminster Abbey. Every so often, Tom would reach into a bag tied to his saddle and sprinkle gold coins among the people standing along the streets. As they scurried for the coins, the people praised the king's name. This made Tom very happy. ''All these people are here to welcome me! *Me!*'' murmured Tom to himself.

As he was about to throw out more gold coins, Tom caught sight of a pale, surprised face peering out from the second row of the crowd. Its intense eyes fastened on his face. It was his mother!

Up flew Tom's hands, palm outwards, before his eyes. When his mother saw this, she pushed through the row of people in front of her and latched onto Tom's leg. "It's you! Oh, my child! My darling boy!"

Tom looked down at her and saw a sweet, loving face brightening with joy. He was just about to let slip the words "I do not know you, woman!" when a soldier came over and pulled the woman off the boy's leg. The soldier sent her hurtling backward into the crowd. As Tom continued forward on his horse, he turned around and saw his mother tearfully staring at him. Her face had a wounded, crushed look.

What have I done? agonized Tom. My own mother! I've rejected her! Have I forgotten my own blood? Ah, I wish I were king no longer!

Tom could not cheer himself as the procession moved forward toward Westminster Abbey. He felt ashamed of what he almost said to his mother, of what he allowed the soldier to do to her. Even as he entered the abbey and knelt before the archbishop, his mind was on his mother. The archbishop was just about to place the crown on Tom's head. Then, a voice pierced the hush in the abbey.

"I forbid you to set the crown of England on that impostor's head. *I* am the king!"

Tom wheeled around. A boy his age, with dirty clothes, emerged from the crowd in the abbey. For the first time in what seemed an eternity, Tom Canty and Edward Tudor were face to face again.

"Seize the beggar!" commanded Lord St. John. "Have him tossed out into the streets!"

"On your peril, Lord St. John," said Tom. "Touch him not. For he is Edward, King of England!" Then Tom knelt before Edward and bowed his head.

Everyone was stunned. No one moved. No one spoke. Indeed, no one knew how to act or what to say. Then the crowd began to whisper. There *was* a striking resemblance between the two boys. Of that, there was no question. But which was king?

"Um, if it please Your Majesty," said Lord St. John first to Tom, then to Edward, then to the space between the two, "I'd like to ask a few questions. They may help identify the true king, for only the real Edward would know the answers."

Both boys nodded their heads. Lord St. John asked Edward many questions about the court, the late king, Princess Elizabeth, and even the prince himself. Edward answered them all correctly. But Lord St. John was still not convinced. He walked closer to the boy in rags.

"Tell me this, then: Where lies the Great Seal of England? Answer me this truly, and the riddle is solved. Only the Prince of Wales would know. On this answer do a throne and a dynasty depend!"

Edward smiled. "There is no riddle, Lord St. John. Go to my private cabinet. On the wall near the floor and by the window, there's a nail head. Press it. A small door will fly open. Inside, you'll find the Great Seal of England."

Lord St. John left the abbey. An hour passed. During that time, the whispering got louder and louder. Even the nobles were shifting their allegiance, siding first with one boy and then with the other. Confusion reigned.

A noise from the rear of the abbey told all that Lord St. John had just returned from the palace. He walked straight up to Tom and stood beside him. "Sire, the Great Seal is not where this beggar said it was," said Lord St. John. "Cast the impostor out and flog him through the streets as a warning to all who dare challenge the king's authority!"

But as two soldiers grabbed Edward under his arms, Tom shouted, "Wait!" Then he looked at Lord St. John. "This Great Seal—is it small and round? And gold? With swirls in it?"

"Of course, Sire, as well you know," replied Lord St. John.

Tom walked over to where the two soldiers were holding Edward. "Unhand him. I command it!" The soldiers let go of Edward. "Now, please think back, Your Majesty, to that time in your chamber. We were standing side by side—remember? And then you dashed out of the room. But before you did, you snatched something from a table and—"

"Hid it in an armpiece of the armor that hangs on my wall!" exclaimed Edward. "The Great Seal of England is there!"

Both boys commanded Lord St. John to search the armor back at the palace. When he returned with the Great Seal in his hand, all knelt down before the boy in rags. A great shout went up from the crowd: "Long live the king!" The shouting and cheering went on for many minutes.

When the noise died down, Lord St. John spoke to the soldiers standing beside Edward. "Take this boy and lock him in the Tower!" He was glaring at Tom now. Everyone was, except Edward.

"Stop!" commanded Edward. "Without this boy, I would not have regained the crown." Speaking more softly, Edward asked Tom, "How did you remember where I put the Great Seal when I could not?"

"Ah, my king, that was easy," replied Tom. "I used it quite often."

"Used it?" said Edward, confused.

"Yes, Sire. But I did not know the Great Seal *was* the Great Seal. You see, I used it for something other than official matters."

"What, pray tell?"

Tom blushed. His eyes dropped to the floor.

"Speak up, good lad," urged Edward. "You have nothing to fear from anyone here. How did you use the Great Seal of England?"

Tom cleared his throat nervously, then said, "To crack nuts with!"

Edward smiled. But the smile faded fast when a loud noise suddenly came from the door of the abbey. Everyone, including Edward, looked back as someone shouted, "I *must* see the king!" Then some soldiers escorted a man to the front of the abbey. It was Miles Hendon!

"Is it you, lad? I've been looking all over London for you since we got separated in the crowd. Are you all right?" Then Miles, looking first at one boy, then the other, said, "For the life of me, I can't tell which is which!"

Edward stepped forward and clapped Miles heartily on the shoulder. "It's me, Sir Miles. I am Edward, King of England. I am the boy whose life you saved. And this is Tom Canty. Like you, he has done king and country a great service."

Miles knelt on both knees before Edward. But the king lifted him to his feet. Kindness and gratitude shone in the boy's eyes. Then Edward caught sight of Sir Hugh Hendon standing among the nobles.

"Soldiers, seize that man!" commanded Edward, pointing at Sir Hugh. "Strip that robber of his false title and stolen estates. Put him under lock and key until I decide what to do with him!"

Sir Hugh Hendon was taken away. Then, Miles saw Lady Edith standing there. Tears rolled down her cheeks. He ran over to her. But before Miles could get a word out, Lady Edith spoke.

"Miles, please forgive me! I had no choice. Sir Hugh said if I didn't deny you, he would take my life. I told him to take it. But then he said he'd take *yours*. And that I could never let happen." She covered her face with her hands. "All these years, Miles, I've loved only you. Can you find it in your heart to forgive me?"

Miles took Lady Edith gently in his arms. "There's nothing to forgive, my love. We're together again. That's all that matters."

King Edward and Tom Canty looked on, beaming.

Hugh Hendon's life was spared. Miles refused to bring charges against his brother. And so Hugh was set free. True to his nature, he deserted his wife and went to Europe. There, he soon died of a mysterious illness.

Not long after learning about Hugh's death, Miles asked his widow for her hand in marriage. Lady Edith eagerly accepted. The two were wed, and their long life together was full of happiness.

John Canty was never heard from again. Mrs. Canty and her two daughters, Bet and Nan, lived with Tom at Christ's Church Hospital. The king had appointed Tom Canty director there. It was a wise choice. Tom took very good care of London's poor, homeless children. Soon his reputation for charity and unselfishness spread throughout London and beyond.

The reign of King Edward the Sixth was short. The boy king would die at a young age. But in the few years he sat on the throne, it was said no kinder king ever ruled England. Edward never forgot the lessons he learned when he was but a pauper in the streets.